The 100% Laugh Riot

Other books you will enjoy

Ask your bookseller for the books you have missed:

PAUL ZINDEL

The 100% Laugh Riot

Illustrated by
JEFF MANGIAT

A SKYLARK BOOK
NEW YORK · TORONTO · LONDON · SYDNEY · AUCKLAND

RL5, 008-012

THE 100% LAUGH RIOT
A Skylark Book / March 1994

Skylark Books is a registered trademark of Bantam Books, a division of Bantam Doubleday Dell Publishing Group, Inc. Registered in U.S. Patent and Trademark Office and elsewhere.

For information address: Bantam Doubleday Dell Books for Young Readers.

ISBN 0-553-48083-9

Published simultaneously in the United States and Canada

Bantam Books are published by Bantam Books, a division of Bantam Doubleday Dell Publishing Group, Inc. Its trademark, consisting of the words "Bantam Books" and the portrayal of a rooster, is Registered in U.S. Patent and Trademark Office and in other countries. Marca Registrada. Bantam Books, 1540 Broadway, New York, New York 10036.

PRINTED IN THE UNITED STATES OF AMERICA

CWO   0 9 8 7 6 5 4 3 2 1

To Marilyn E. Marlow

Contents

THE WACKY FACTS LUNCH BUNCH OATH

We, the undersigned, vow to make our fifth grade at New Springville Elementary School cram full of laughs, good times, and mind-boggling adventures—and be the best of friends until death do us part!

Signed in bloodred barbecue sauce,

*Dave Martin*_____, **PRESIDENT**, in charge of *Wacky Facts* and *warp speed action!*

*Liz McGinn*_____, **EXECUTIVE SECRETARY**, specializing in *Knock-Knock jokes, horrifying headlines,* and *secret club notes.*

*Johnny Hayes*_____, **VICE PRESIDENT**, in charge of *Goony Gags, puzzles,* and *"Really Freaky Things to Do"!*

*Jennifer Lopez*_____, **TREASURER**, in charge of *"Ghoulie Foolies," tongue twisters, money-making ideas,* and *healthy food!*

*Max Millner*_____, **OFFICIAL CLUB ARTIST**, specializing in *hilarious cartoons* and *excellent funny jokes.*

The 100% Laugh Riot

►ONE◄

Buenos Días, Baby!

Monday morning all the kids in Mrs. Wilmont's fifth-grade class freaked out the second they walked into her room!

"There's the Creature from the Black Lagoon!" I yelled.

"Oh, Dave," Max laughed, "you always zero in on the wacky stuff!"

Mrs. Wilmont had cut out pictures of famous actors, dancers, and singers and taped them all over the blackboard!

"What's going on, Mrs. Wilmont?" I called out, forgetting to raise my hand.

"I'm glad you asked, Dave," she said. "I cut out these pictures of performers to get the class in the mood."

"In the mood for what?" Jennifer wanted to know.

"Well, I was wondering how you would like to put on a *talent show*." She ran her hand through her short brown hair.

"Yes!" I called out right off the bat. **"I could stand up at a microphone and tell really weird facts like how some kid in Florida sued his parents for nicknaming him 'DOPE-ON-A-ROPE'— and how a teacher in California saw poltergeists blow up a toilet bowl!"**

"A *stand-up Wacky Facts act* is a great idea, Dave," Liz said. "I could sing a song from *PHANTOM OF THE OPERA!*"

"Terrific, Liz," Johnny agreed, "and while you're singing, I could lope around onstage dressed in a mask and drool fake blood."

"Thanks, but no thanks," Liz groaned.

"I'll do a great modern jazz ballet!" Jennifer bubbled.

Max's eyes opened as wide as a pair of CDs. "I can do scribbles on a big pad and have the audience guess what the scribbles are supposed to be. I did it once at a birthday party, and it went over huge! Although I might think of something else."

As usual, the Wacky Facts Lunch Bunch got everyone worked up.

"We'll do a rap!" the Jocks said.

"Maybe we'll sing a rock song as a group!" the head of the Stuck-ups, Wendy Potts, volunteered.

"We've been practicing precision basketball dribbling," a girl Jock called out.

"I think those are all wonderful ideas," Mrs. Wilmont agreed.

"We can run up a wall!" Nat Bronski called out.

"Yeah," his buddy Rado Clapp agreed.

"How do you do that?" Mrs. Wilmont asked, puzzled.

"We run really fast along the floor," Nat explained. "Then, when we reach a wall, we run up it really high before we drop down onto a mat."

"Oh, my," Mrs. Wilmont said, "that does sound different."

"Yeah, it'll be a showstopper!" Nat promised.

The whole class talked at once.

"I'll do card tricks!"

"I'll do spins on Rollerblades!"

"I'll play my electric guitar!"

"I'll play my violin!"

Mrs. Wilmont blew her whistle.

"WEEEEEEEEEEEEEEEE!"

Everyone snapped to attention.

"I'm glad you're all so excited," she said. "A lot of the other classes have already done their Community Service Project for the term. Now it's our turn. I've already spoken to the **New Springville Senior**

Citizens' Home. They said they'd love to have us do a talent show for them."

Jennifer raised her hand. "I remember that place. When we were in the second grade we were all bussed over during the holidays to sing 'O COME, ALL YE FAITHFUL' and 'CHANNUKAH, O CHANNUKAH.'"

"Those old people were all bored out of their minds," Rebecca Barnes, one of the girl Jocks, said. "We'd get more applause if we put our talent show on at the mall. At least we'll get an audience with a heartbeat!"

Rebecca Barnes has a special talent for saying exactly the wrong thing at the wrong time, which is why our code name for her is *PECKY*, not Becky.

"I assure you the SENIOR CITIZENS are very excited about our class coming," Mrs. Wilmont said. "The director of their Social Committee, Isabel Zaks, called me this morning to say they even want to award a prize to the best act in our show."

"Like what?" practically the whole class asked at once.

Mrs. Wilmont smiled. ***"A SUPER TREAT BASKET packed with things like hand-dipped chocolates, candies—and a coupon book of movie passes to the CINEPLEX! Also, the winner will get his or her picture in the newspaper!"***

"I'd love my picture in the paper," I said.

"Me, too," Jennifer agreed.

"I want the movie passes," Liz admitted.

"*When* do we put on the show?" Rebecca Barnes asked.

"We go at the end of the week," Mrs. Wilmont said.

"*THIS* Friday?" I asked.

The class went bananas.

"WEEEEEEEEEEEEEEEEE!" Mrs. Wilmont let her whistle rip, and the class quieted down fast. "Each of you can show off your best *ready* talent. Nothing has to be perfect," she said reassuringly. "I can accompany anyone on the piano who needs it."

"I think what those senior citizens really need are laughs!" I said. "My grandfather Jack is seventy-two years old, and he zooms around Daytona Beach on a motorcycle. He picks up babes his age and hits the comedy clubs."

Jennifer rolled her eyes. "Get real, Dave. You can't expect those kind of people at the old folks' home in New Springville."

"My aunt's mother is eighty, and she's still a blonde. She used to be naturally blond, but now it's out of a bottle," Wendy Potts volunteered.

"My neighbor's mother is ninety, and she likes to play the slot machines in Las Vegas!" Johnny laughed.

"That's what I'm saying," I said. "Our show has

to have a lot of action and be really funny, or these old folks are going to nod out!"

"Running up a wall is funny!" Nat called out.

"We need to be MORE than funny," I insisted.

Mrs. Wilmont pursed her lips. "We only have a few days, Dave. I'll be glad if everyone participates and it turns into a nice program."

"We've got to have that audience rolling in the aisles," I explained.

"The only rolling in our aisles is going to be done by wheelchairs," Rebecca complained. "That place is Zombie Central!"

"That's why we've got to give them the best show we can!" I said. "We need to really blow their minds!"

"Hey, we're supposed to entertain them, not give them cardiac arrest!" Liz scolded, starting to chew on her hair.

"I remember a lot of them knitting during 'O COME, ALL YE FAITHFUL,'" one of the nerds said.

Suddenly, my brain got so excited I couldn't stay in my seat. *"I know exactly what kind of a show they need!"*

"Get to the point, already," Jennifer said, clicking a ballpoint pen like a machine gun.

"We need to put on a real side-splitting show!" I said. "We've got to throw pies! Wear big shoes and red rubber noses! We've got to be

clowns with our pants falling down! We need globs of funny, really unexpected stuff! That's the kind of talent show we have to give them! *A 100% WILD AND FREAKY LAUGH RIOT TAL-ENT SHOW!*"

The Abominable Pickle!

The bell rang for lunch, and the whole class went ballistic out into the halls. We headed down the stairs to the cafeteria like chickens with our heads cut off.

"We've got to come up with a really hilarious act," I told the Wacky Facts Lunch Bunch, taking two steps at a time.

"Great!" Max said.

Johnny laughed. "Party! Party!"

"I don't think I can be *hilarious*," Liz moaned.

"Me, either," Jennifer said.

When we reached the cafeteria, we zipped straight for our WFLB table. We have the best table near the windows and farthest away from the steam table, which always has a special for the day that looks like pickled fish lips.

"I found a book on magic that shows how to make a chicken disappear," I said. "It's all done with mirrors."

"Maybe we should wear bathing suits and lip-sync to one of the Beach Boys' surfer tunes," Johnny suggested.

"Or the Rolling Stones," Max said.

"I can lip-sync the lead singer of any group," Liz offered.

"We could be mud-wrestling coneheads!" I suggested.

"BOOOOORING," Jennifer moaned, tossing her head. Her long, black ponytail swung behind her and smacked Rebecca Barnes's left ear. It was weird because Rebecca always sits with the girl Jocks, but today she was at the Supernerds' lunch table right behind us.

"Ow!" Rebecca screeched.

"Oops! Sorry," Jennifer said.

Rebecca spun around in her chair. When she saw what hit her, she let loose one of her big phony smiles.

"That's okay, Jennifer," she said.

Pecky is always easy to spot because she has a mop of frizzy red hair that looks like she is the Bride of Frankenstein and has been struck by lightning. I read in a magazine that the world record for being struck by lightning really is held by a shepherd on the island of Sardinia. He was hit eleven times and lived!

Pecky turned back to the nerds as though she were interested in them.

"Why is PECKY sitting there?" Liz whispered.

"I don't know," Jennifer whispered back.

"I overheard the girl Jocks saying they might end their basketball dribbling routine by forming a human pyramid," Max said.

Johnny started munching one of the two mega meat sandwiches oozing with brown gravy that his mother always packs him.

"Maybe we should do gymnastics," Jennifer said, opening a plastic container of small mozzarella cheese globs. "I can walk on my hands." She plopped a mozzarella glob into her mouth and started chewing.

"Yuck! It looks like you're eating cow eyeballs!" Johnny complained.

"It's a lot healthier than that cholesterol festival going on in your mouth," Jennifer shot back.

Jennifer's mom and dad own a grocery store, so it's easy for her to bring stuff like dried figs, mangoes, and nuts. Liz, Max, and I always buy our lunch, so we hit the food line fast and headed back with pizza and drinks. As President, I called the Wacky Facts Lunch Bunch Club to order immediately.

"We're all agreed that we want to win the talent show, right?" I asked, pulling a gooey string of melted cheese off my chin.

"It'd be great if we got our picture in the paper," Johnny said.

"I'd really like that," Liz admitted.

"Okay," I went on, "but what we've got to do is plan our own terrific LAUGH RIOT. We'll be so funny all the senior citizens will vote for us, and we'll win the Super Treat Basket hands down!"

"What will we do—split everything?" Max asked.

"Yes," I said.

"I don't want any fudge or junk food," Jennifer told them, "but what if there are only four movie passes? Which of us doesn't get one?"

Liz sucked up her milk through a straw. "What if there are like seven pieces of homemade fudge and thirteen chocolate chip cookies and nineteen candies and seventeen movie passes? How do we split it all without getting into a fight?"

"What if the basket is a nice straw one?" Jennifer asked. "Who gets to keep the basket?"

"We can draw straws," Liz said, laughing.

"What we've got to talk about is our act," I insisted. "The way I see it is that I'll be the Master of Ceremonies for our WFLB section of the program. I'll come out and say something like, *'Hello, everybody! Did you know that in May 1987 a crazed wife in Paris, France, terrorized her husband by tying him up and pressing giant toads on his face?'* "

"You're going to freak the old people out!" Jennifer gurgled, shoving another cow eyeball into her mouth.

"You don't like Wacky Facts anymore?" I asked.

"Sure, we like them," Jennifer said. "I'm just saying we can't tell old folks in rocking chairs a lot of shocking things and think they're going to give us first prize in a talent contest! Besides, Wacky Facts are interesting, not HILARIOUS!"

"So, I'll find hilarious ones! Besides, I'll only be warming them up," I explained.

"Why don't you warm them up with KKs?" Liz suggested.

"No way," I said.

"Knock, knock." Liz started her own favorite kind of joke anyway.

"Who's there?" Max played the straight guy.

"Orange juice," Liz said.

"Orange juice WHO?"

"Orange juice sorry you made me cry?"

Liz was the only one who laughed. "All right, so you guys don't think it's very funny," she said. "I've got lots of others. Our audience will like them, and then I'll sing. In fact, Jennifer and I could do a number together!"

"I don't know," Jennifer said. "But I do think we could use the new Ghoulie Foolie I brought in for today's meeting. See, this hairy, drooling werewolf with big fangs walks into a Baskin-Robbins ice cream parlor and orders a sundae with vanilla ice cream and butterscotch syrup, topped with whipped cream, sprinkles, and a cherry—"

"I heard this one," Johnny garbled with his mouth full.

"Then stick grapes in your ears," Jennifer said, rolling her eyes. "So this kid soda jerk makes the sundae for him—but the werewolf notices the kid staring at him while he's gobbling it up, and the drooling werewolf says to the kid, *'What're you looking at? You think it's freaky that a werewolf would come into a Baskin-Robbins and order an ice cream sundae with vanilla ice cream and butterscotch syrup, topped with whipped cream, sprinkles, and a cherry, eh?'* And the kid says, *'Actually, no. I like it that way myself!'* "

"Is that the whole joke?" I asked.

Jennifer glared at me. "Of course it's the whole joke!"

"That's more revolting than the wife pressing toads on her husband's face!" Liz complained.

"I don't even *get* the joke," Max said.

Jennifer huffed. "It's not a *'JOKE'* joke. It's like a humorous story, and it'll make everyone smile."

"It didn't make ME smile," I said. "What we need to figure out is what we're all going to do together to stop the show! I've got a Mandrake the Magician book that shows how to saw somebody in half. Johnny could be the top part of the body. Liz could be the legs."

"Double bore," Jennifer moaned.

"Hey, it's a terrific idea," I insisted.

Liz scrunched up her face. "Dave, I don't want to play a couple of sawed-off legs. I'd rather sing a song."

"Look, guys," I reminded everyone, "we've got a club here. Whatever we do, we're certainly going to do it together."

"What could I do in the act?" Max asked.

"You hold the saw and then hand it to me for the cutting part," I said.

Max frowned. "That's *all*?"

"You can also walk around and let members of the audience feel the teeth of the saw so they know it's for real," I suggested.

"I'd rather tell jokes," Max said. "I could open our act by asking the audience if they know why Cinderella was thrown off the baseball team . . ."

"Jeez," Jennifer complained, "everyone knows it's **BECAUSE SHE WAS AFRAID OF THE BALL!** I'd be careful with a joke like that. The girl Jocks might not like it and cream your butt."

"Just because YOU know the answer doesn't mean the whole world knows it," Johnny said, standing up for Max.

"Right," Max said. "Besides, I've got a lot of other

jokes—I'm more than just an artist. Did you hear about the cross-eyed teacher they fired yesterday? They had to—he couldn't control his pupils!"

Liz laughed. "I like that one."

"I think I should open the show with *this*," Johnny said, holding up a banana.

"A banana?" Max exclaimed.

"Are you out of your gourd?" Jennifer asked.

"It's a special banana," Johnny said. "Look, it's presliced! Honest!" He started peeling the banana. We all freaked when we saw it really was already *SLICED* inside!

"How did you do that?" I really wanted to know.

"It's easy," Johnny said. He fished a needle and thread out of his backpack. "See," he said, "you just stick the needle through a flat section of the un-peeled banana. Then you do the same thing for the other flat sections all around the banana, and when you pull on the thread, it makes a slice INSIDE the unpeeled skin. You sew the thread into the banana and pull it for as many slices as you want."

Suddenly, a grating voice interrupted us.

"Jennifer, I was really glad to hear you might be going to dance in the talent show," Pecky, the Bride of Frankenstein, cackled.

"Thanks, Rebecca," Jennifer said in a polite voice.

"We're glad Jennifer's going to dance, too," I

said. No matter what, the Wacky Facts Lunch Bunch stick together.

Rebecca flashed another phony smile and turned back to chat with the nerds.

"What's she up to?" Liz whispered.

"I don't know," Jennifer said.

We all knew PECKY well enough to know she doesn't do or say anything unless there's something in it for her. Maybe she was going to use the Supernerds for dumbbells.

"Look," I told Liz, lowering my voice, "after I have 'sawed off' your legs, you can climb out of the box and sing **'I AIN'T GOT NOBODY!'** Get it? **NO BODY!** It'll be a scream!"

"Then sing it yourself! I need a HONEY RICE KRISPIE and another milk," Liz moaned, getting up and heading for the food line.

Liz wasn't gone a second before Rebecca Barnes spun back around from the Supernerds' table again and hopped her chair right next to Jennifer's.

"Jennifer, can I talk to you a minute?" Rebecca asked, her voice sounding like sandpaper scraping across concrete.

"Sure," Jennifer answered.

Johnny, Max, and I made believe we were going on with a regular dumb conversation, but we were really listening to hear what Rebecca was going to lay on Jennifer.

"You know, Jennifer," Pecky said, "you're really the best dancer in the school."

"Thanks," Jennifer said, her face growing a little rosy. "You're a very good dancer, too."

"Well, that's exactly what I was thinking," Rebecca added.

"WHAT were you thinking?" I interrupted.

Rebecca gave me a BUTT OUT smile, like if I didn't she was going to sock me. She went right on blabbing to Jennifer. "Liz is such a good singer that if she does a solo, I guess she'll win the talent show—unless you come up with a really great dance."

"I was thinking I might do something with heavy-duty gymnastics in it. I'm not sure about the music yet," Jennifer said.

"Have you noticed how anybody who dances in the Miss America Contest always loses out to the person who belts out a song? I happen to remember the interpretive modern jazz dance you did last year in the fourth-grade show. I thought you were terrific, but let me tell you, everybody else liked Liz singing 'CLIMB EVERY MOUNTAIN' better."

"They did?" Jennifer whispered. "Rebecca, what are you trying to say?" she pressed, drumming her fingers on the table.

"I learned a fun dance at summer camp," the Bride of Frankenstein continued. "At the camp talent show, everyone loved it and clapped for ten minutes."

"That's great," Jennifer said. "So do it in the talent show."

Rebecca sighed. "I would love to, but it's much better with two people in the spotlight. I was thinking—we haven't danced together, but we're both so talented that if you and I did it together, we would win and get our picture in the newspaper."

"I don't think so, Rebecca," Jennifer said.

"I'll show you the way it starts," Rebecca insisted, standing up. "It seems silly at first, but I know the old people will adore it. It is called THE KANGAROO HIP HOP!"

Johnny, Max, and I looked at each other as Rebecca started dancing and singing right in front of us: *"Do the Kangaroo! Do the Kangaroo! Listen and I'll show you how to do the Kangaroo!"*

Rebecca took Jennifer's hand and pulled her up next to her. "Come on. It's a real cute dance. We'll dress in orange leotards and tights and wear pointy headbands for ears . . ."

"I can't," Jennifer said.

"Sure you can," Rebecca insisted. She got behind Jennifer and put her hands on her hips. "It's like the Bunny Hop, but better! *First you rock it to the left, then you roll it to the right! Then you hip hop! Hip hop! with all your might!* Every senior citizen knows the Bunny Hop. They will vote for us."

Jennifer looked like she felt really stupid as Rebecca made her follow the steps. Jennifer learns things fast, though this was a dance an idiot could pick up in two seconds.

Rebecca sang on, *"That's what you do when you do the Kangaroo!"*

"I feel funny," Jennifer said, looking around the cafeteria but not at us.

"You're doing great," Rebecca encouraged, and then started making Jennifer jump all around the place with her. **"HIP HOP, HIP HOP . . ."**

The nerds started humming along as Rebecca began the stupid song and dance all over again. This time Jennifer sang a little and danced along with Rebecca. Jennifer's voice sure helped a lot. What surprised us was that half the kids in the cafeteria started to clap along.

Liz came back from the food line and sat down. She had bought *two* HONEY RICE KRISPIES. She placed one on the table in front of Jennifer's empty chair.

"Pecky coming over here and making Jennifer dance is creepy," I told her.

Johnny agreed. "I'd like to know who besides Pecky in their right mind would want to hip hop like a kangaroo!"

"I don't know," Liz said, *"but from the looks of things, I'd say we're losing Jennifer from our act."*

THREE

Tooth and Consequences!

After school I went straight home to check my Man-drake Book of Magic. It had great diagrams to show how to construct a setup to make audiences think I was actually sawing somebody in half! All I would need were two orange crates.

That night at the dinner table I discussed my idea to saw somebody in half with my family.

"I want to saw somebody in half, too!" my eight-year-old sister Giggles said, laughing and munching on Chinese pea pods. Her real name is Gillian, but one of our baby-sitters called her Giggles, and the nickname stuck for good reasons.

"Dave, won't sawing someone in half be too grisly for a talent show?" my mom asked.

"It sounds like it's right up Dave's alley—nice and freaky," Dad said.

"Can I saw *YOU* in half?" Giggles asked me, and she giggled so hard she started to choke.

Mom tapped her gently on the back and made her take a sip of water. "It's not nice to saw people in half," Mom said, shooting me a look to change the subject.

"You want to hear one of Liz's KNOCK-KNOCK jokes?" I asked my sister.

Giggles giggled. "Yes!"

"Okay," I said, "but first tell me, would you remember me if I left tomorrow and went to live in Borneo with a tribe of mutant cannibal Pygmies?"

"Yes!" Giggles said. Suddenly, she looked worried. "Please don't go. Don't go live with PIG-MEEZE."

"Dave, I thought this was going to be a KNOCK-KNOCK?" Mom shot me another famous look.

"And would you remember me if an albino alien with claws and webbed feet takes me away in a UFO?" I kept staring at Giggles.

"Sure," Giggles said.

"Will you **ALWAYS** remember me?" I dropped my voice to make it sound really spooky. Even Darwin, our Great Dane, wondered what was going on and snuggled his head into my lap. The only time he usually does that is when he eats fish or a greasy bone and wants to wipe his mouth off.

"Yes, Davy," Giggles promised, "I'll remember you always and always and always!"

"KNOCK, KNOCK!" I said suddenly.

Giggles looked puzzled. "Who's there?" she asked anyway.

"What?"

"Who's there?" Giggles repeated.

"Giggles, I thought you said you'd ALWAYS remember me!" I complained.

Mom and Dad laughed.

It took about ten seconds for Giggles to get the joke. Sounding like a tickled hyena, she smacked corn kernels around on her plate.

After dinner I dialed Liz's number to see if she had any great ideas about how to make her part in being sawed in half hilarious.

"Hello," she answered the phone.

"Hi, Liz," I said. I could hear her eating popcorn.

"Hi, Dave."

"We need to talk about the Wacky Facts Lunch Bunch act for the talent show," I went on.

"Dave, I'm sorry," Liz said. "I've decided I'm going to sing a Broadway show song—maybe 'MEMORIES' from *CATS*."

"Great idea," I agreed. "I'll start sawing away, and the audience will hear this singing coming out of your box with only your feet sticking out of it. It'll be like you're singing 'MEMORIES' to your legs. It'll be a scream!"

"No," Liz said. "Listen to me . . . I'm going to sing my song alone—standing up, holding a mike, like a real performer."

"What?"

"I talked it over with my mom, and she thinks old folks will really enjoy it," she said.

"But we're a club. We're best friends and pals," I reminded her. "We have to come up with something we can all do together."

"Jennifer's not going to be available, either." I heard Liz shoving a big handful of popcorn into her mouth. "She just called to tell me she's definitely doing THE KANGAROO HIP HOP with Rebecca Barnes."

"You're kidding!" I gasped.

"No, I'm not."

"THE KANGAROO HIP HOP is completely goony!" I freaked. "I'll call Jennifer. She'll change her mind."

"I'm still doing 'MEMORIES' alone," Liz said. "I really want to."

"Sleep on it," I suggested.

I hung up and dialed Jennifer. She answered the phone on the extension in her parents' grocery store.

"What's up?" she asked. "I can't talk long. I'm helping my mom and dad stick prices on figs."

"Is it true you're going to do THE KANGAROO HIP HOP with Rebecca Barnes?" I asked directly.

"Yes."

"Are you nuts?"

"Dave, it's a cute act."

"For morons."

"Dave, I really like it. It's going to please our audience."

"Rebecca Barnes doing anything is not cute. It's nasty! She's using you."

"She is not."

"Of course, she is," I insisted. "Rebecca knows if she got up alone, they'd bring out a hook and yank her off the stage like a sack of potatoes. She thinks if she does the dance with you, nobody'll notice she's got three left feet and hair like a nuclear carrot!"

"Dave, if you'll excuse me," Jennifer said, "I really have to get back to the figs."

She hung up. I called Johnny.

He answered the phone in his room. I explained the act.

"I have to stick my head out of an orange crate?" he asked.

"Yes," I said. "It'll be a scream!"

"How is my sticking my head out of an orange crate going to be a scream?" Johnny wanted to know.

Suddenly an idea hit me. That's how my mind works. One minute I don't know what I'm doing, and the next I can see things plain as day.

"Say, you know that song 'THAT'S *AMORE*'? You know . . . 'WHEN THE MOON HITS YOUR EYE LIKE A BIG PIZZA PIE, THAT'S AMORE'?" I asked.

"My grandmother likes that song. It's for old people. What about it?"

"Well," I said, "I was thinking that we could play that song while you're in the box, and when the guy sings 'WHEN THE MOON HITS YOUR EYE LIKE A BIG PIZZA PIE,' Max could run onstage dressed like a chef with a real pizza in his hand and plop it on your face!"

"A *hot* pizza pie on my face?"

"It doesn't have to be hot."

"I don't want globs of tomatoes and cheese up my nose."

"There won't be globs up your nose," I insisted.

"I don't think a pizza pie in *my* face is funny," Johnny complained. "Besides, Rebecca Barnes talked to me at the end of the day. She said she thought I really should come up with my own **REALLY FREAKY THINGS TO DO** act. She wants me to go before she and Jennifer do THE KANGAROO HIP HOP."

I thought I was hearing things.

"The Bride of Frankenstein spoke to you, *too*?"

"Yes."

"Actually, Rebecca wondered why you wanted to

snatch the spotlight away from me in the REALLY FREAKY THINGS TO DO department."

I was so furious at Pecky Barnes I couldn't talk.

"Dave, are you still there?" Johnny asked.

"Yes," I finally said.

"So I think I'll just do my own thing, okay?" Johnny added.

"Okay," I muttered.

After I hung up, I went downstairs to the kitchen and had a frozen candy bar and a humongous chocolate milkshake to cool down. Then I called Max. I wanted to make sure *he* was still in the act.

"The senior citizens are going to be really interested in feeling the teeth of the saw to make sure it's a real saw," I said. "It's a very important part of the act. You can even say things like 'WATCH OUT YOU DON'T CUT YOURSELF ON THE RAZOR-SHARP TEETH.'"

"I don't want to walk around with a saw that has razor-sharp teeth," Max said as if he were just waiting to tell me.

"They'll really be dull teeth!" I exclaimed.

"Look, Dave," Max said, "I might as well tell you that somebody said I really should think about doing a STAND-UP COMEDY act on my own for the show."

"The Bride of Frankenstein spoke to you!"

"Yes," Max admitted. "Rebecca really sounded

worried about me making a fool of myself. Would you mind if I tell jokes alone? I'd really rather do that."

What could I say but okay? Obviously, the Wacky Facts Lunch Bunch weren't going to have any act together for the talent show. *The only thing I WAS sure of was that somehow, some way, I was going to get even with Pecky Barnes for making me into a laugh riot of ONE!*

►FOUR◄

Aagh! Aagh! Aagh!

The next morning I stopped by Liz's house so we could walk to school together, like we usually do. When she wasn't waiting outside, I rang the front door bell.

Liz's mom opened the door. She was dressed to go to work. Mrs. McGinn is a court stenographer. She always keeps her eyes open for special legal Wacky Facts for me, like how the French government is being sued for using helicopters to drop millions of frozen medicated fish balls over the countryside to protect foxes from rabies, and how it's illegal to hunt mongooses on Saint Thomas.

"Oh, Dave!" Mrs. McGinn said. "I'm sorry, but Liz left for school already."

"That's okay."

"Will you be able to catch up with her?" she asked.

"No problem," I said.

I took the shortcut from Glen Street to Richmond Avenue. I didn't see Liz.

A block from school I saw Jennifer going in the main entrance gate.

"Hey, Jennifer," I called, even though she was too far away to hear me. She disappeared inside.

Only Max was waiting for me by the time I reached school. The Wacky Facts Lunch Bunch always meets in the auditorium at 8:30 A.M. sharp. Then we go up together to work on Mrs. Wilmont's lab squad.

"Everybody else went on to the laboratory supply room," Max said.

"Oh."

We started up the stairs.

"I hope we don't have to deliver a lot of equipment this morning. I didn't get much sleep," Max added.

"I didn't sleep so great, either," I said.

"Good morning," Mrs. Wilmont said cheerfully when we walked into the lab supply room.

"Good morning," Max and I said back.

"Hello," Liz mumbled as she was putting together an equipment order for Mrs. DiGiuseppi's class. It was a bunch of metal rods, a coil of wire, and an electric generator that you crank.

Johnny gave a wave as he was setting up a plastic model of the human brain for Mr. Breiden's class.

"Hi, Johnny," Max said.

Jennifer was dusting off a jar brimming with embalmed grasshoppers, which made me feel like tossing my sugar-frosted breakfast.

"Hi." Jennifer smiled.

Mrs. Wilmont is in charge of all the science equipment for the school. Our WFLB volunteered in September when she said she needed help filling teachers' orders and delivering the equipment. We get to use a lot of the scientific gizmos and gadgets while we earn service credits. We also figured it would be a good chance for the WFLB to spend more time together.

"Why so glum?" Mrs. Wilmont asked as she put her arm around the laboratory's human skeleton. "You're all as lively as Mr. Bones here. You usually come in and can't wait to tell me your latest joke. What's the problem?" She can read us like a book.

"Well," Jennifer said, "Dave wants the Wacky Facts Lunch Bunch to do an act together for the talent show, but it's not working out that way."

"Let me see if I've got this straight. Each of you wants to do a solo act—is that it?"

"Except for me," Jennifer said. "I want to do THE KANGAROO HIP HOP with Rebecca Barnes.

She and I have been jazzing it up, so we think the old folks will really enjoy it!"

"Dave, why do you object to the others doing something on their own for a change?" Mrs. Wilmont asked.

"We could all saw someone in half *together*," I explained. "The whole reason we formed the Wacky Facts Lunch Bunch in September was so we could do things together!"

Jennifer rolled her eyes. "I think that Dave thinks Rebecca Barnes is trying to break up our club."

"You bet I do," I admitted.

"Look, Dave," Mrs. Wilmont said, "regardless of what Rebecca Barnes wants, don't you think sometimes it's good for each of you to do something on your own?"

"We could really win the talent contest if we all stuck together," I answered.

As Mrs. Wilmont took her arm down from Mr. Bones she turned to me.

"Dave, you must have noticed that a great many of the most important accomplishments in the world have been achieved by people who dared to think and act alone. That's not to say they didn't have friends or belong to clubs, too. Where would we be if Columbus, Einstein, and even Elvis Presley had just always gone along with the crowd?"

"Rebecca Barnes just wants to split up our club," I said.

"Look," Mrs. Wilmont said—her voice was kind, but her words stung—"the most important thing is that each of you not let your individualism interfere with your friendship for each other. Value yourselves as well as your club. No matter what you decide to do in our talent show, I want you to remember one thing . . ."

"What?" Max asked.

"It's important to be strong enough to do your own thing and stand out from a crowd!" Mrs. Wilmont said. "Just think about that!"

Mrs. Wilmont waved her hands. **"IT'S FINE TO STAND OUT FROM A CROWD!** Let's repeat it, this time louder, like a cheer." I had kept my mouth shut because I didn't feel like being a phony. "And you join in, Dave!"

I went along with the others, just to make Mrs. Wilmont happy:

"IT'S FINE TO STAND OUT FROM A CROWD!"

I knew then and there that it was going to be easier said than done!

► F I V E ◄

Chop Shticks
and Scream Gems!

The bell rang at 9:00 A.M. We went to class.

As we walked through the hallway, I noticed that Johnny's backpack had an extra bulge in it that I knew had to be more than a couple of juicy roast beef sandwiches. Max was studying his sheet of jokes as we walked. Liz and Jennifer looked like they were daydreaming about the talent show. Everybody in the WFLB acted like they were on completely different wavelengths—which I was afraid of all along.

"Hi, Jennifer!" Rebecca Barnes's grating voice said the second we walked into the class.

"Hi, Rebecca!" Jennifer said cheerfully.

The Bride of Frankenstein gave me a humongous smile. I gave her a snort.

"Her hair is extra big today," Liz whispered to me.

"Yes," I agreed. "It's like a giant furry eraser."

Mrs. Wilmont has plants on her desk and the best aquarium in the whole school.

"We'll hold rehearsal third period," Mrs. Wilmont said, walking to her desk. "It's the only time the auditorium is free today, and we'll need the piano."

"JENNIFER AND I ARE GOING TO GET THE MOST APPLAUSE! JENNIFER AND I ARE GOING TO GET THE MOST APPLAUSE!" Pecky did it SINGSONG, like she was still in kindergarten.

The way Liz glared at Pecky made me think she really wanted to sock it to Pecky as much as I did.

First period was math. Then in history Mrs. Wilmont told us a mind-boggling story about Hannibal. She said in the third century Hannibal led his army and a herd of elephants over the Alps to fight the Romans.

"Remember *your* elephant ride at Zoo Habitat?" I asked Mrs. Wilmont.

Mrs. Wilmont laughed. "I certainly do!"

I knew nobody would ever forget our class trip to the New Springville Zoo Habitat when an elephant ran off with Mrs. Wilmont, Liz, Johnny, and Max sitting on top of it.

"I was just as surprised by that ride on an elephant as I'm sure the Romans were when they saw

Hannibal attacking them with his elephants!" Mrs. Wilmont added.

"That's what we need for Pecky Barnes," I whispered across the aisle to Liz.

"What?" she asked.

"A really good surprise attack!" I said.

Liz winked back.

At 11:10 A.M. Mrs. Wilmont took the class to the auditorium. Except for Jennifer, the WFLB all sat together. I think she would have sat with us except that the Bride of Frankenstein yanked her down in a seat next to her.

"Attention! Attention, everyone!" Mrs. Wilmont called out as she walked to the piano. "We've got a lot of work to do, so let's get started. I need a volunteer to take notes for me as we plan our show."

"Can I take the notes?" Tommy Russo, head of the Supernerds, called out, waving his hand like a pom-pom. "Can I?"

"Yes," Mrs. Wilmont said, handing him a pad and pencil.

"Brownie points!" Nat Bronski shouted.

"We decided that senior citizens probably like DOO WAH music, so we're going to be the **DOO WAH** GIRLS," Wendy Potts said. She stood up and gave Mrs. Wilmont sheet music as the rest of the Stuck-ups giggled like crazy.

"What are DOO WAH GIRLS?" Johnny asked.

"My neighbor told me she was once on the great stage. They go *'DOO WAH'* when they sing," Wendy explained in a voice that seemed to say he was just one of the most unbearable geeks on our planet.

Mrs. Wilmont sat down at the piano and started to play.

The music wasn't too bad, but once the Stuck-ups warbled, " 'BOBBY THRILLS US SO, DOO WAH, DOO WAH . . .' "—half the kids fell on the floor, laughing.

Wendy didn't laugh. She just said, "Wait until you see our poodle skirts—you'll all be jealous and we'll win."

The Blobs started their act next.

"Watch how we run up the walls!" Nat Bronski yelled.

"Wait!" Mrs. Wilmont ordered. "Get a mat from the gym."

"We don't need one," Rado squeaked, and instantly he and Nat ran at top speed to a tile wall near the stage. They got about six feet high before they fell to the floor with a **THUDDDDD!** They bounced up, grinning. "We'll run even higher on Friday for the senior citizens!" they promised.

"I'm sure they will appreciate that," Mrs. Wilmont said, "but make certain we bring a mat with us."

I raised my hand.

"What, Dave?" Mrs. Wilmont asked.

"I think *I* should be the Master of Ceremonies," I told her.

"Dream on!" Rebecca called out. "I think I'M the one who should be the M.C."

"But Dave does bring up a good point," Mrs. Wilmont said. "I think we should have a Master or Mistress of Ceremonies. Raise your hand if you would like to be considered for the job."

I shot up my hand at the same time Pecky shot up hers.

We were the only ones.

"All right," Mrs. Wilmont said, "since there's only Dave and Rebecca who want the job, how about Dave being the M.C. for the first half of the show, and Rebecca can M.C. the second half!"

"Great," I said. "Getting the show off to a dynamite start takes the most talent."

"That's a laugh!" Pecky said. **"You can make the first half into one big joke. Everyone knows that the most important, serious performers of any show appear in the second half."**

"We're going to have wonderful acts all through our show," Mrs. Wilmont said. ***"Everyone will be a star. Now, who wants to rehearse next?"***

"Can I go?" Johnny asked.

"Certainly," Mrs. Wilmont said.

"The ***REALLY FREAKY THING TO DO*** I would like to use in my act is THIS," Johnny said.

Every one of us looked surprised when Johnny took a shoe box out of his backpack. He walked up front. It had holes in the top.

"What is it?" Liz asked.

"It's a SHOE BOX CONSTELLATION," Johnny answered.

"What's that?" a nerd called out.

Johnny opened the box. In it was a flashlight, which he clicked on. He put the lid back on the box. When he held it against a wall, it made lights on it, even in the daytime. The lights were in the formation of THE BIG DIPPER.

"This is just one of my shoe box constellations," Johnny explained. "But for the show I'm going to make other shoe boxes to show **THE LITTLE DIPPER, TAURUS THE BULL, LIBRA THE LION, CAPRICORN THE GOAT,** and lots of others. First, I'll announce that I am going to take the audience out of this world in broad daylight!"

"What an imaginative thing to do," Mrs. Wilmont said.

"Should I write down SHOE BOX CONSTELLATIONS to be in the show?" Tommy Russo asked.

"Yes," Mrs. Wilmont said. "By all means."

Johnny sat down with a smile on his face. "I think I'm really going to win the Super Treat Basket and get my picture in the newspaper," he whispered to Rebecca.

"You are out of your mind." Rebecca Barnes leaned forward.

Robert Warner stood up with the other boy Jocks and explained, "We started working on our rap, which we wrote ourselves."

"Yeah!" the other Jocks agreed, falling all over each other, laughing.

"Let's hear what you've got," Mrs. Wilmont said. The Jocks stood up and rapped:

We saw an old guy who had a big nose,
That hung to the floor like a long garden hose.
Blowing his nose was really a bore,
So he sat on down, threw a fit on the floor . . .

Half the kids in the class cracked up. Everyone looked to see what Mrs. Wilmont thought.

Finally, she said, "I suppose even Shakespeare had to start somewhere! I really want you to change 'OLD GUY' to 'YOUNG GUY.' Since we are going to be performing for nice older folks at the senior citizens' home, we need to be sensitive to their feelings. The rest of it I'm sure they'll understand. After all, they were young once."

Liz went next. She gave Mrs. Wilmont her sheet

music for "MEMORIES." When she hit the high notes at the end, everyone applauded.

"Your voice gets more beautiful every year, Liz," Mrs. Wilmont said. "I really do think the senior citizens are going to be very, very moved by your song."

"Thank you," Liz said, obviously proud of herself, and sat down.

"That was really lovely," Jennifer told Liz. "I thought I was listening to the radio or a CD."

"Thanks," Liz said.

"I hope you don't get so nervous you blow it," Pecky whispered to Liz. "You'll chew on your hair, and your voice will crack during the real show. Besides, 'MEMORIES' is yesterday's news. Maybe you should reconsider and pick something more up-to-date."

Liz didn't even answer Pecky.

Rebecca jumped up and gave Mrs. Wilmont her sheet music for THE KANGAROO HIP HOP. Jennifer was on her feet, holding on to Pecky's hips. They looked like a locomotive and a caboose. They hopped all over the place, singing the dumb song, but Jennifer had added a lot more jazzy steps, and her voice sounded great, too. Lots of kids applauded them.

"We are going to win. It's in the bag," Pecky gloated as she went back to her seat.

"Your head is in a bag," I told her.

The five nerds went next. Their act was a version of THE LYING GAME where they said they were going to each tell the audience one fact, but one of them was going to be lying. It would be up to the audience to tell which one it was. The whole idea was so lame that half the class didn't want the act in our show.

"It's low key but asks for audience participation," Mrs. Wilmont said, encouraging the Supernerds. "I think the senior citizens will appreciate a nice, quiet routine like that."

Richard Wood, the head Zombie, stood up. "We want to recite the poem 'The Raven' by Edgar Allan Poe."

"That's a fine idea," Mrs. Wilmont said.

"We haven't memorized any of it yet, though," Richard muttered.

"Just get to work on it tonight," Mrs. Wilmont suggested.

Next the girl Jocks did a precision basketball dribbling routine, while Mrs. Wilmont played "STARS AND STRIPES FOREVER" on the piano.

Max's turn was next. He stood in front of the group. Max has stage presence—that's how he won class rep.

"Hi, folks," he said, talking to us like he was really doing the show. *"You know, a funny thing happened to me on the way over here to the New Springville Senior Citizens' Home. I stepped on a*

bunch of grapes and they let out a little <u>whine</u>. Get it? Then I came across a very frightened tree. It knew that it was scared because it kept telling me how <u>petrified</u> it was. But I always say a tree is like a computer. Smash a computer and let the chips fall where they may . . . !"

Pecky Barnes stared at Max like she thought he had lost his marbles. "That's an act we don't have to worry about," I heard Pecky whisper to Jennifer.

"He's a *good* stand-up comic," Jennifer said, defending Max.

"Max, those are super jokes," Mrs. Wilmont said.

"I've got a million of 'em!" Max told her.

"What a big bore!" Rebecca groaned.

I raised my hand. *"Can I have Max in the first half of the show that I M.C.?"*

"Is that all right with you, Max?" Mrs. Wilmont checked.

Max looked happy. "Sure."

"I *would* like to make one little suggestion . . ." I said.

"What?" Max asked.

"Your jokes are funny," I remarked, **"but at the end of your act, I think I should throw a cream pie in your face!"**

Mrs. Wilmont raised her eyebrows. "I am sure Max would not care for that!"

"The audience would howl," I said. "How about it, Max?"

"Hey," Pecky brayed, "our audience is old, not loony tunes."

"Maybe the senior citizens *would* get a laugh out of it," Max said.

"It's the perfect touch. Trust me. Okay, Mrs. Wilmont?" I asked.

Mrs. Wilmont winked. "Who am I to stand in the way of artistic expression."

"Why doesn't Dave show us what great act he's going to do in the show, or is he just going to throw the bull as an M.C.?" Pecky called out.

Mrs. Wilmont gave Pecky a "CHILL OUT" look.

"Oh, I'm doing an act, all right," I said, giving Pecky the evil eye.

"What is it?" Mrs. Wilmont asked.

"It is spectacular!" I announced without even thinking. *"Something that has never been done in the history of all show business. Something so mind-boggling it will really be a total razzle dazzle riot!"*

"What?" everyone wanted to know.

In the second that followed, the thought suddenly came to me.

"I'm going to saw MYSELF in half!" I said. **"Yes, that's what I'm going to do! *I WILL SAW MYSELF IN HALF!*"**

Mrs. Wilmont looked surprised.

"Saw yourself in half?" she asked.

The whole class had eyes the size of radar dishes.

Pecky howled.

"Dave, is that what you are *really* going to do?" Mrs. Wilmont asked.

"Yep."

I couldn't stop my mind from going ballistic. Within two seconds, I was MORE than excited. I thought up my most mind-boggling idea of all. *The fat, juicy cream pie was NOT going to end up in Max's face! There would be a pie flying through the air at the talent show, all right, but somehow, some way, I personally was going to see to it that the pie would land smack on Pecky Barnes's head!*

► S I X ◄

Schemin' Demons!

By the end of school that day the members of the Wacky Facts Lunch Bunch were at least talking to each other again. We even went out the front gate together.

"Hey, Dave, when are you going to bring your act in?" Johnny asked.

"Thursday," I said.

Max looked surprised. "You are going to wait until the day before the show?"

"I have to build the coffin that I'm going to cut in half with me inside," I explained. I did not want to admit I had just thought of the idea that day.

"A coffin is creepy," Liz said. "Why can't you just call it a 'magic box'?"

"No matter what I call it, it will still look like a coffin," I explained. "Mandrake the Magician said half the fun for an audience is when you make any trick you do look mysterious."

"A coffin may be mysterious, but it doesn't sound like a laugh riot to me," Jennifer said. "And what will the old people think?"

"I'm going to decorate the outside of the coffin with magic symbols like the Romans used to use on their shields to repel Evil!" I added.

"Are you going to let out make-believe screams while you're sawing?" Jennifer asked.

"Sure," I said. "That's show biz."

"Are you going to have a balloon filled with red Kool-Aid inside so when you cut it, it will look like an explosion of blood?" Johnny asked.

"No," I said. "Everyone will know it's Kool-Aid."

We stopped on the corner.

"I wish you luck with your dance," Liz told Jennifer.

Jennifer gave Liz a hug. "You sounded great singing 'MEMORIES'! I think you're going to win the Super Treat Basket and have your picture all over the papers. Maybe a talent scout will discover you for the movies!"

"Thanks," Liz said. "I'll be happy if any one of us in the WFLB wins."

Jennifer had to go help out at her parents' grocery store. After that she takes care of her "MUTTS BY THE MILE" dog-walking service.

"Oh, I have a new client," Jennifer called over

her shoulder as she started down the street. "It's a German police dog that looks just like Rin Tin Tin. It belongs to one of the ladies who shops at our store."

"Congratulations!" Liz called after her.

"I guess I have to go home now, too," Max said. "I need to dig up a few better jokes."

"If I come across a real side-splitter, I'll call it in to you," Johnny offered.

"Me, too," I promised.

Johnny had to go home to mind his two younger brothers and work on his shoe box constellations. That left only Liz and me, so we started walking home past Ronkewitz's Candy Store.

"At least everyone seems to be chillin'," I said.

"I am not chillin' over Rebecca Barnes," Liz growled. She nibbled on her left knuckle. "I hope a sixty-ton meteor crashes into her bedroom tonight and liquefies her."

"I hope a tornado sucks her up and sets her down in a freezing mountain pass so she has to eat snow and spiders to survive," I said. "That's what this one fifteen-year-old boy had to do last winter in Colorado."

"I want someone to put a voodoo curse on her and turn her into a tree," Liz added. "I'm sorry, but that's how I feel."

I laughed. "I can tell you something that *IS* going to happen to her."

"What?"

"You know my cream pie?"

"Yes," she said.

"Well"—I smiled—"it's going to collide with the Bride of Frankenstein's mug!"

Liz looked at me.

"How?" she asked.

"Easy," I said. "I'll tell Max to run when he sees me heading for him with the pie at the end of his act. He can just happen to be running accidentally-on-purpose by Pecky Barnes when I throw the pie."

"Max will duck, and the pie will fly into Pecky's face?"

"Right!"

"That's horrible," Liz said.

"Yes! The Bride of Frankenstein is going to get slimed."

"Can I make the pie?" Liz pleaded.

"Would you?"

"Yes! Oh, yes!" Liz cheered. "If anyone deserves a pie in the face, it's Pecky Barnes!"

"What should we put in it?"

"Gross stuff," Liz urged.

"Like what?"

"My mom has heavy-duty paper plates left over from last summer," she said. **"That will let us have a nice big pie and we won't have to throw a real plate. All we want is some good**

cream fun! And I could make a bottom layer of peanut butter, topped with molasses . . ."

"My father has Gorgonzola cheese." I snickered.

"What's Gorgonzola cheese?"

"It smells like up-chuck!"

"Nice." Liz giggled.

"I read an article about one cheese they make in Switzerland that is aged in horse manure. I wish we had some of that."

Liz gagged. "Dave, you made that up."

"No," I said. "It's a fact."

Liz started to skip along the sidewalk. "I'll top the whole pie off with a mountain of whipped cream."

I started to jog to keep up with her. "Beat the cream good, so it stays really thick," I suggested.

"You bet!"

"We could use old, soggy coffee grinds in it, too," I added. "I knew a kid at camp last summer who did that, and the counselor hung him up on a nail by his underpants!"

"Coffee grinds are a nice touch." Liz laughed as she skipped faster and faster.

We were still laughing when we reached Liz's shortcut to Glen Street.

"Bye, Dave!" Liz said, running off toward her house.

"Bye, Liz!"

I headed for Victory Boulevard and straight for the supermarket. The manager, Mr. Carter, is really nice and always gives kids empty boxes for things like school projects and go-carts. He let me pick out two neat orange crates. They were really light, so I had no trouble carrying them home.

"What are you going to do with those?" Giggles asked as I marched the crates in the front door.

"Nothing," I said.

"Can I help you do nothing, DAVEEE?" Giggles giggled.

"Did you have your cookies and milk yet?" I asked.

"No."

"You should go help yourself," I told her, "and then you could start your homework. Mom will be home soon."

"Okay, DAVEEE!" Giggles laughed and scooted for the kitchen.

I brought the crates up to my room and shut the door. The wood on them was so thin I had no trouble cutting out the holes I needed with a pair of my dad's linoleum shears. The hardest part was attaching the bottom of the crates to a couple of my old skateboards, but a couple of old leather belts took care of that nicely.

After dinner when my mother was cleaning up, I asked, "Mom, do you have any old bedspread or cloth you don't need?"

"Look downstairs in the basement. I have a rag bin next to the washing machine," she said.

"Thanks."

"There are some old towels and curtains," she called after me, "and I'm throwing out the purple shower curtain with the yellow fish all over it!" My mom works in the Classified Ads Department at the *New Springville Tribune,* but she always has time to help me with special projects.

"Wow!" I called up. "Fish have always been magic symbols!"

"By the way," Mom said, coming to the top of the stairs, "I noticed in the newspaper two articles you'll love. In the science section, I read that the Egyptians put brass balls in the eye sockets of their mummies, and when I read the style section it mentioned that the bread PUMPERNICKEL was named after Napoleon's favorite horse, Nicoll. I marked the pages for you!"

"Thanks!"

I brought the shower curtain up to my room, cut it, and stapled it onto the orange crates. When I finished that, I went to talk to my dad.

He was in the living room, vibrating in his massage chair. Giggles and Darwin were with him, watching a rerun of *ALFRED HITCHCOCK.*

"What's up, Dave?" he asked.

"What's up?" Giggles repeated.

"Not much." I whispered in my father's left ear,

hoping Giggles would not be able to hear. ***"I need to make a pair of fake legs."***

"What are you talking about?" he whispered back.

"I told you, I am going to saw myself in half for the talent show," I explained. "I need two fake legs to push out of one of the crates so they look like they are my own."

"Oh."

"Daddy," Giggles cried out, pointing at the TV screen, "here comes the part where the woman hits the man with the frozen leg of lamb!"

"Yes, honey," Dad said. "Close your eyes."

"I want to see," Giggles insisted.

"How would *you* make fake legs?" I continued whispering into Dad's ear.

"Hmmmm . . ."

"Got any ideas?" I asked.

"I think so," he said finally.

"What?"

"I've got a couple of SHOE TREES in my closet," Dad said. "You know, those wooden foot-shaped things I put in my good shoes?"

"Yes," I said.

"You can stuff them in a pair of your sneakers," Dad advised, "and make them stick out from the bottom of a pair of jeans."

"Cool."

"And stuff the jeans with newspaper so it looks

like there are really legs in them." Dad sounded like he was really getting into it.

"Great, Dad."

"Anytime."

I started out of the room.

"DAVEEE!" Giggles called after me, **"I was listening! I was listening! DAVEEE! Make me a pair of fake legs, too!"**

Hurrah for Howlywood!

Wednesday morning a messenger from the MAIN OFFICE delivered a note to Mrs. Wilmont's classroom. We were in the middle of art, but all the kids stopped to watch Mrs. Wilmont tear open the envelope.

"Oh!" Mrs. Wilmont cried out as a bunch of sparkling colored confetti popped out and fluttered down to the floor.

"Who sent you confetti?" Liz asked.

"Yeah, who?" a nerd echoed.

Mrs. Wilmont looked really puzzled as she lifted a note out of the envelope. It was dripping with confetti!

"It has got to be from a real banana!" Nat shouted.

"Why, no!" Mrs. Wilmont exclaimed. "It's from

Mrs. Zaks and the rest of the Social Committee at the SENIOR CITIZENS' HOME."

"What does it say?" the Bride of Frankenstein asked.

"Is the show canceled?" Johnny sounded worried.

"Why, no," Mrs. Wilmont said. "I'll read you the note."

> *Dear Mrs. Wilmont and students,*
> *We wanted to tell you how much we look forward to the talent show this Friday! We are very excited and cannot wait. We will have microphones and anything else you need. Just let us know. The Super Treat Basket has grown into something wonderful. We think the winner of the talent show will be very pleased with it. We're ready for action! Break a leg!*
> *Best wishes from the Social Committee! Isabel, Estelle, Herb, Sol, Murray, Helen, and Dolly*

"Way to go," Max said.

"Sending confetti is weird," Pecky said.

"I think it is sweet and imaginative," Mrs. Wilmont corrected her.

* * *

By Wednesday night I felt good about my act. I practiced sawing myself in half a half-dozen times in my room. It worked great. I still wanted to talk to my friends. I figured I could get everyone to liven up the show. My nickname wasn't ACTION DAVE for nothing!

I dialed Jennifer first. She answered in her family's apartment above the store.

"What, Dave?" She sounded suspicious.

"I just wanted you to know there is time for you to nix THE KANGAROO HIP HOP. You can help me during my act. While I saw myself in half, you could do cartwheels and double splits next to me!"

"Are you out of your mind?" she asked.

"No," I answered. **"After I have finished sawing myself in half, you can roll the box with my feet away from the box with my head and do a double flip."** I heard her suck in air.

"I am sticking with THE KANGAROO HIP HOP," she said.

"Didn't you get into a million fights with Pecky Barnes yet?" I really wanted to know. "Don't you think she's just using you?"

"You can ask her yourself, Dave," Jennifer said. "She's right here."

A lump formed in my throat as I heard the phone being passed.

"Hello, Dave . . ." The Bride of Frankenstein's scratchy voice crawled out of the receiver.

I wanted to drop the phone and throw up.

"Oh, hi, Rebecca," I said, swallowing hard.

"Have you got a problem?" she asked.

"No, I do not have a problem but you do." I took a deep breath and decided not to be a big phony. "Look," I said, "I called Jennifer to let her know it's not too late for her to cancel doing THE KANGA-ROO HIP HOP with you. Give the audience a break!"

"Do you really hate the dance that much?" the Bride asked.

"You want the truth?"

"Yes," Pecky said.

"It's a real stinker."

"We disagree with you!" her voice screeched from the phone. "Our dance is going to be a hit, and we'll be in the newspaper next to the lotto numbers. Page One."

"Rebecca, your dance is going to bomb!"

"Dave, do me a favor and saw yourself in half at the neck right now," Pecky suggested. "Even Jennifer's mother said THE KANGAROO HIP HOP is going to be a smash."

"It's for dweebs!"

"No, it's not!" Pecky went on. "Jennifer's mom

informed us that what we call THE KANGAROO HIP HOP is just like a dance they still do in South American countries and at high-society parties in the U.S. of A. Have you ever heard of a 'CONGA LINE'? Hundreds of people get up on the dance floor with the music playing, and in a long line, they go 'ONE, TWO, THREE, KICK! ONE, TWO, THREE, KICK!' The only reason you don't know about it is because your brain is wacky!"

"Look, Rebecca, I actually have heard of a Conga line. I know plenty of Wacky Facts. But a HIP HOP is *not* a Conga line." I said. "I just don't want you to make my pal look like a Kangaroo dork next to you."

Pecky snorted. "You're just jealous that Jennifer and I are going to *win* the talent show."

"THE KANGAROO HIP HOP couldn't win a freak show!"

"Oh, shut your face!"

"Hey . . . !"

Pecky hung up.

I was fuming so much I went downstairs to the kitchen and drank three huge glasses of Gatorade to cool off. It took me ten minutes before I was able to dial Liz's number.

"Hello." Liz answered the phone and she didn't even have popcorn in her mouth, because her voice was clear.

"I just called Jennifer. The Bride of Frankenstein was over there rehearsing with her," I said.

"What happened? You sound mad."

"Jennifer put the Bride on the phone."

"And?"

"Let us put it this way," I said. ***Is everything all set with the pie?***

"Not exactly," Liz said. "My mother says the pie should only be whipped cream so it's easy to clean up."

"I guess we can live with that—but make it extra double thick!"

"You got it!" Liz promised.

I hung up from Liz, and called Johnny. He was busy working on the SCORPIO THE SCORPION constellation and said he would call me back.

Last, but not least, I dialed Max.

His father answered the phone, which always scares me a little because he sounds like an uptight vampire. Of course I never mention anything about it to Max because I don't want to hurt his feelings.

Max got on.

"Are you still doing your stand-up comedy act?" I asked.

"Yes," Max said. "Did you come up with any side-splitters?"

"Yes."

"What?"

"Pecky Barnes is going to get the pie in her face, not you," I said.

"I like that joke," Max said. "That is what I call a really funny punch line!"

"Me, too," I had to admit. "I like it a lot! Here's my plan. . . ."

Thursday's final rehearsal in the auditorium came so fast I got spaced out. Mrs. Wilmont made me bring in my orange crates so she could see what my act was going to look like. I just went through the motions slowly. I didn't want to show all the tricks up my sleeve because then everyone would know how mind-boggling it was really going to be.

"Dave, do you want me to play any background music while you saw yourself in half?" Mrs. Wilmont asked.

"Yes."

"What would you like?"

"Do you know **'BEAUTIFUL DREAMER'**?" I asked.

Mrs. Wilmont looked surprised. "That is such a lovely, sweet piece of music. What made you pick that?"

"It's the music they play in the movie *MIGHTY JOE YOUNG*," I explained. *"You know, he's a giant ape like King Kong, and they capture him and bring him to the city where he goes berserk and destroys a big, fancy nightclub that is decorated with live lions and tigers."*

"Oh," Mrs. Wilmont said.

"Is Dave still throwing that stupid pie in Max's face at the end of Max's act?" Pecky Barnes inquired like I was not even in the auditorium.

"Are you, Dave?" Mrs. Wilmont asked.

"You bet!" I said. I gave Pecky a little wink, and added, "It is going to be something really special."

At the end of rehearsal, Mrs. Wilmont gathered us around her at the piano. "I would like to go over a few last thoughts about things we might run into with our audience."

"Like what?" Nat yelled out.

"I want you prepared for the fact that some of the senior citizens may want to shake your hands," Mrs. Wilmont began. "Some of them might be in wheelchairs or on crutches. A few might even need to take your arm to sit down. Things like that."

"No strangers are going to lay a hand on me," Rado bellyached.

"Each of you can do what you are comfortable with," Mrs. Wilmont said. "Some of you might like to bring photos of pets or of your younger brothers and sisters."

"Hey," I called out, "we don't want to scare them to death!"

Everybody knows Giggles, so they laughed.

"No, we do not," Mrs. Wilmont agreed. "Our project is to show we care for others. These older folks are going to love all of you kids—you'll remind them of youth and energy. I wanted you all to know some of them might pat you on the head or even show you pictures of their own grandchildren and pets they once had."

"So what?" a nerd asked.

"Well," Mrs. Wilmont continued, "sometimes a visit from a class of young people can make the older folks nostalgic. Some might get tears in their eyes or even weep for a moment."

"I went to visit my great-grandmother in a senior citizens' home once," Wendy Potts said, "and one of the old ladies wanted me to buy a potholder she made."

"Thank you for sharing that with us," Mrs. Wilmont said.

"I am not buying any potholders!" Nat yelped.

"I am certain that was an unusual circumstance," Mrs. Wilmont remarked. **"What the senior citizens are going to adore is each of you taking the time to come visit and perform for them. Just get out there and give it your best shot,"** she continued, but now she sounded like a baseball coach. "Remember the spirit of S.H.A.R.E.! You are to be commended for this community service! Some of you have heard me say IT IS FINE TO STAND OUT IN A CROWD! Now is your chance—and may the best act win!"

EIGHT

Showtime!

Friday morning I had the most stuff to load on the CLASS TRIP BUS to the New Springville Senior Citizens' Home. Johnny and Max helped me with the orange crates. Liz looked great. She wore a white dress and had tied back her hair. She carried the pie. Her mom had lent her a great hatbox to carry the pie in so it wouldn't get squished.

The second the Bride of Frankenstein got on the bus, she headed straight for me.

"Can I see the pie?" she asked, showing off her red, white, and blue costume. She had put silver sparkles in her hair, so she looked like a giant patriotic strawberry ice cream cone with weird sprinkles.

"Sure," I said. "Take a good look!"

Pecky stared into the hatbox at the mountain of luscious whipped cream.

"It's a big pie," Pecky said, "but still it's going to be a really humongous bore to hit Max in the face. Big Deal."

"Let me know after the show," I suggested.

Pecky laughed right in my face. "Oh, Dave, I won't have time for that," she said. "Jennifer and I will be too busy eating the treats from the Super Basket and posing for photographers!"

"NOT!" I said.

Mrs. Wilmont did a final attendance check, and the bus pulled away from the school. It was only a ten-minute ride to the Home, but it was too far for the class to walk with all the props.

"ATTENTION! ATTENTION!" Mrs. Wilmont called out, turning to face us from the seat next to the bus driver. "Here's the final lineup of the acts," she said. She passed down mimeographed sheets to everyone.

"Good," Pecky called out. "I have the best acts to M.C. in the second half of the show!"

"I'm glad I'm in *your* half of the show," Liz told me. She sat next to me as the bus bounced along.

"Thanks," I said.

"I wouldn't want to be in Pecky's half," she added, starting to chew her hair.

Nothing on the mimeographed sheet was a surprise to me since I had handpicked all the acts I wanted to M.C., and Mrs. Wilmont had okayed them. At least I would introduce all of the WFLB acts except for Jennifer and Pecky's. All the Bride of Frankenstein fought for was that she and Jennifer close the show with THE KANGAROO HIP HOP! Jennifer was all done up in red, white, and blue, too. On Jennifer it looked sharp.

"We're in the best spot to win the talent show," Pecky told Jennifer nice and loud so everyone on the bus could hear it.

The whole class went ballistic when the bus turned off Forest Avenue and pulled up in front of the Senior Citizens' Home. A gang of senior citizens were standing out in front waving like crazy and holding a giant computer printout:

WELCOME MRS. WILMONT AND HER FIFTH GRADE CLASS!

"Who are they?" a Supernerd asked.

"The Welcoming Committee," Pecky crowed. "Just part of the crowd who is going to vote for Jennifer and me!"

The bus doors opened with a **SWUUUUSSH!**

Mrs. Wilmont was the first one out. The rest of the class struggled after her with the props.

"Careful with the pie!" I told Liz.

"No problem," she said, carrying the hatbox like it had a priceless jewel in it.

The Welcoming Committee rushed Mrs. Wilmont and our class. Everyone started shaking hands and introducing themselves to us a mile a minute.

"What a pleasure to meet you, Mrs. Wilmont," one smiley lady with blue-gray hair called out. "I'm Isabel Zaks! We're so thrilled you and your class could come!"

"We're so pleased to be here," Mrs. Wilmont said as the Committee began to herd us in through the front doors of the Home. The building looked just like I remembered it when we sang there in the second grade. It had a new canopy out front, but it was still modern with a lot of glass.

"I'm Herb," a friendly bald guy with a limp and a beer belly told me. "You know, this Home used to be a Holiday Inn!"

"That's interesting," I told him.

A couple of other men with gray hair insisted on helping with the orange crates. A few senior citizen ladies helped the other kids with their stuff, too.

"I'm so nervous," Liz whispered to me as she clung to the hatbox.

"Don't worry," I said. "The worst that could happen is you'll get a terminal case of stage fright and pass out on stage."

"David, that is not funny," Liz moaned, giving me a little kick.

"Only kidding," I said.

It seemed to me that all the kids except for me and the Bride of Frankenstein looked nervous. Some kids tripped and dropped stuff as we went through two sets of glass doors.

"Where are we going to do the show?" Max asked.

"They have a big rec room," I told him.

Isabel dashed by me, making a weird CLICKING noise. She sounded like a roller coaster.

"What is that noise?" Johnny asked, struggling with his shoe boxes.

"I think that old lady Isabel has taps on her shoes," I said.

"What for?" Liz wanted to know.

"Maybe she's on a limited income, and it makes her shoes last longer," I said. "Lots of old people don't have a lot of money, you know."

The two guys carrying my orange crates introduced themselves.

"I am Sol," the tall one said.

"I'm Murray," the short one said.

Sol and Murray together looked like the comic strip characters Mutt and Jeff.

One woman with big bleached blond hair gave me a humongous hug as we were marched into the main rec room.

"My name is Helen," she told me.

"I'm Dave," I said.

"I'm really super nervous now," Liz groaned at

the sight of the stage. It was more like a raised dance floor, but there were more than a hundred other senior citizens already sitting on folding chairs waiting for us.

"Nobody is playing checkers or knitting!" Max exclaimed.

"They all look wide awake," Liz said, starting to chew a new section of her hair.

"We thought the kids could all get ready here," Isabel said, indicating a bunch of empty seats behind a big screen.

"This will do fine," Mrs. Wilmont said.

"Hi, everybody!" some woman called out with a booming voice. She wore boots and a frilly vest like she was a mature cowgirl. "I'm Estelle," she said. "Did you like the confetti in our note? It was my idea!"

"It was a wonderful surprise," Mrs. Wilmont told her as she checked out the piano in front of the screen. "I hope you don't mind if I borrow the idea and start putting confetti in some of the letters I send!"

"Be my guest, honey," Estelle said.

Estelle sat down in the front row. In a flash, Isabel clicked her way into the seat next to her. Also in the front row were Herb with the beer belly, Sol, Murray, and Helen with the bleached blond hair.

"When are you going to start the show?" a

woman who looked like the Wicked Witch of the West yelled out.

"Hold your horses, Dolly," Isabel told the Witch. Then Isabel called to us, "Don't let Dolly scare you. She has a heart of gold."

Suddenly, everyone in the room went silent except for the first row, which was still gabbing away. The hundred other senior citizens all looked nice and normal like a regular audience.

"You can start when you're ready, Mrs. Wilmont," Isabel said.

Mrs. Wilmont peeked behind the screen. "Are you ready, Dave?" she asked.

"Ready!"

"Good luck, kids," Mrs. Wilmont said, running her hands quickly through her hair. She went to the microphone.

"Ladies and gentlemen!" Mrs. Wilmont announced. **"My class and I are very pleased to be with you this morning. The kids have worked very hard all week, and I know you're going to enjoy the show . . ."**

"So start it already!" Dolly the Witch blurted out.

I thought Mrs. Wilmont was going to reprimand the Witch, but she didn't. **"It gives me great pleasure,"** she said, **"to introduce the student M.C. for the first half of our show—Dave Martin!"**

Mrs. Wilmont scurried to the piano and played

some great chords as I ran out from behind the screen. At least a hundred of the senior citizens really looked distinguished and applauded.

"HI, FOLKS!" I said into the mike. "YOU KNOW, WHEN THE SOCIAL COMMITTEE SENT US A NOTE FILLED WITH CONFETTI, I COULDN'T HELP BUT REMEMBER THE UNUSUAL FACT THAT OAK TREES ARE STRUCK MORE BY LIGHTNING THAN ANY OTHER KIND OF TREE."

I had everyone's attention. This was going to be a piece of cake.

"I COLLECT WACKY FACTS, AND THERE ARE A LOT OF THEM ABOUT SENIOR CITIZENS," I continued. "DID YOU KNOW THAT ON APRIL 23, 1993, A SEVENTY-THREE-YEAR-OLD DENTIST BUNGEE-JUMPED OFF A BRIDGE? AND JUST LAST JULY, A SIXTY-EIGHT-YEAR-OLD GRANDMOTHER SAVED A POODLE FROM THE JAWS OF AN ALLIGATOR AT A GOLF COURSE!"

Everyone still looked like they were enjoying my Wacky Facts. The only senior citizens who were rustling were the members of the Social Committee in the first row.

"Enough with the weird facts already!" Dolly the Witch screeched.

"Hey, give the kid a chance," Herb told her.

I figured I had better move the show along, anyway.

"Pssssst!" I whispered to Liz. "Are you ready?"

She nodded *yes.*

"IT GIVES ME GREAT PLEASURE NOW TO INTRODUCE OUR OPENING ACT, LIZ MCGINN, SINGING THE HIT SONG FROM CATS, 'MEMORIES'!" I said.

"Thanks, Dave," Liz muttered as she took over the mike.

"Take your hair out of your mouth," I whispered, and went behind the screen.

"Ha!" Pecky Barnes gloated to me. "They didn't laugh once."

"They were all very interested," I said. One look at Pecky's face reminded me to check the hatbox to make sure the pie would be handy when I needed it. I also checked out my orange crates and cutting saw. I didn't want anything to go wrong when it was my turn.

"Will you need me to help push you out in the crate?" Johnny asked.

"No, thanks," I said. "I have that part all worked out."

Max rushed over. "What is that CLICKING sound going on during Liz's song?"

Johnny, Max, and I peeked out from behind the screen.

"It's Isabel," I said.

She was sitting tapping her foot to "MEMORIES." Every time her foot hit the floor, there was a CLICK. Liz looked freaked. I figured it wouldn't have been so distracting if Isabel hadn't been sitting in the front row. Estelle was playing with the frills on her cowgirl vest and patting her left knee in time with the music. Herb, Sol, Murray, and Helen were doing their share of twitching, too.

"I don't get it," Johnny said. "All the members of the Social Committee look like they're in costume."

"They probably just dress weird," Max said.

Liz got a nice round of applause when she finished. She rolled her eyes toward the first row as I scooted by her back to the mike. I knew what she meant.

"MOVING RIGHT ALONG NOW, FOLKS," I said, "THE FIFTH GRADE IS PLEASED TO PRESENT JOHNNY HAYES WITH A REALLY HEAVENLY ACT!"

Johnny ran out with his arms filled with shoe boxes. He tripped on the mike cord and some of the tops fell off.

"WHILE WE'RE WAITING FOR JOHNNY TO SET UP," I continued, "I KNOW YOU'LL ALL BE INTERESTED TO KNOW THAT AS OF 1992 THERE ARE MORE THAN FIVE THOUSAND MAN-MADE OBJECTS FLYING IN SPACE! ALSO, DID YOU KNOW THAT THE SUN BURNS NINE MILLION TONS OF GAS A SECOND!"

"That's almost as much gas as YOU!" Dolly called out.

The whole audience laughed.

I didn't think it was very funny. I could tell by the expression on Mrs. Wilmont's face that she didn't appreciate the remark either. She started to play "STARDUST" as Johnny took over the mike and held up his first shoe box.

"FOR MY FIRST CONSTELLATION," Johnny announced, "I WOULD LIKE TO SHOW YOU **PEGASUS THE HORSE** . . ."

"Oh, quit horsing around!" Dolly shouted right off the bat, and let out a shriek of laughter.

I disappeared back behind the screen to make certain Max would be ready to go on next. We needed laughs bad.

Liz rushed to me. "They hated me," she cried, nibbling her right knuckle.

"No," I told her. "The applause was really loud."

"The only thing loud was Isabel's *CLICKING*!" Liz said.

Max ran over to me and Liz. "Johnny is bombing out there!"

I peeked around the screen. The whole audience looked restless, even the normal senior citizens. I let Johnny do CANCER THE CRAB, but in the middle of CAPRICORN THE GOAT, Dolly started yelling, *"GET THE HOOK! GET THE HOOK!"*

I looked to Mrs. Wilmont. She stopped playing

"STARDUST" and motioned me to take over the mike.

"WELL, THANK YOU, JOHNNY, FOR YOUR TERRIFIC SHOE BOX CONSTELLATIONS!" I said.

"Thanks for rescuing me," Johnny said, scooping up his shoe boxes and fleeing offstage.

"NOW, FOLKS," I said fast, "HERE IS MAX MILLNER, ONE OF THE FINEST UP AND COMING COMEDY STARS OF NEW SPRINGVILLE ELEMENTARY SCHOOL!"

Max dashed to the microphone.

"GOOD MORNING, LADIES AND GERMS!" Max said loud and clear. "HA! HA! I MEAN, *GENTLEMEN*! A FUNNY THING HAPPENED ON MY WAY OVER HERE—I HEARD A FIFTY-CENT PIECE AND A QUARTER THREATENING TO JUMP OFF THE VERRAZANO BRIDGE. OF COURSE, I KNEW THE QUARTER WOULD JUMP FIRST BECAUSE IT HAS LESS SENSE. HA! HA! GET IT?"

The audience looked at Max like he had just escaped from a nuthouse. Only Sol and Murray had smiles on their faces.

"MOVING RIGHT ALONG," Max charged on, "I GUESS A LOT OF YOU KNOW THAT A TOUPEE AND A SECRET HAVE A LOT IN COMMON."

"Yeah," Murray called out. "You keep both of them under your hat!"

The audience roared.

"You tell him, Murray! You tell him!" Dolly yelled.

Max forced a smile and continued. "YOU KNOW, FOLKS, I WAS GOING TO BRING MY PET FROG IN WITH ME TODAY TO DO SOME JUMPS FOR YOU—"

"But he woke up sad and *unhoppy*!" Sol shouted.

The whole audience laughed again, but practically everyone in the first row fell off their chairs.

Max looked to Mrs. Wilmont. She got up from the piano bench and went to the mike. **"KINDLY GIVE EACH OF MY STUDENTS THE ATTENTION HE OR SHE DESERVES,"** she announced. She made it very clear she was talking to the first row, because the rest of the senior citizens were really a great and terrific audience.

"Keep going," she whispered to Max, and scooted back to the piano.

"YOU KNOW," Max said, staring right at Sol and Murray, "YOU TWO REMIND ME OF A COUPLE OF RODEO MEN!"

"Because we are always throwing the bull!" Sol and Murray said together like they were a vaudeville team.

The audience roared with laughter again.

I ran out on stage and took the mike from Max. "LISTEN, IF YOU TWO GUYS THINK YOU CAN

DO ANY BETTER, WHY DON'T YOU COME UP
AND TRY IT!"

I couldn't believe that Sol and Murray got out of
their seats and came right up onstage next to Max.

"I beg your pardon," Mrs. Wilmont said, ticked
off, "but my student is not finished yet!"

"We just want to help him out," Sol said, putting
an arm around Max's shoulder. "Say, Max," he said,
"do you know the difference between a mouse and a
beautiful girl?"

Max's face turned stark red. "No."

"Well," Murray jumped in, "the mouse harms the
cheese, and the girl charms the he's!"

Everyone in the audience laughed their heads
off.

"You know, Max," Murray continued, "do you
know why a steam locomotive doesn't like to sit
down?"

"Beats me," Max admitted.

"After all," Sol said, taking over, "a locomotive
does have a tender behind."

Even the kids in our class laughed at that one.

Mrs. Wilmont charged the stage. "Thank you for
your contributions to our show," she said, taking
Sol and Murray by their arms. She escorted them
quickly back to their seats.

"Do a last joke," I called to Max as Mrs. Wilmont
went back to the piano.

"DO YOU TWO GUYS KNOW WHAT YOU WOULD HAVE IF A BIRD GOT CAUGHT IN A LAWN MOWER?" Max shouted at Sol and Murray.

The audience waited, but Sol and Murray did not know.

"SHREDDED TWEET!" Max said with a huge smile, and ran off.

"You forgot to throw the pie, dummy!" Pecky laughed at me.

"Don't call Dave a dummy," Liz stood up for me. Then she whispered in my ear, "Dave, you DID forget the pie!"

"I know," I admitted. "I got confused!"

I ran out and grabbed the mike.

"AND NOW, LADIES AND GENTLEMEN, WE BRING YOU THE RARE TALENTS OF NAT BRONSKI AND RADO CLAPP!"

Mrs. Wilmont started playing fast, loud circus music. Nat and Rado ran out with their mat and started running up the wall on the other side of the stage. Even the first row was stunned into silence.

"Hey, we're climbing the walls around here, too, you know!" the Wicked Witch of the West blurted out.

The audience started laughing again, but Nat and Rado's act was over in a flash.

"ATTENTION! ATTENTION, PLEASE!!" I blasted into the microphone. "YOU ARE ABOUT

TO SEE ONE OF THE MOST ASTOUNDING FEATS OF MAGIC EVER ATTEMPTED!"

I set the mike down on the floor and ran back behind the screen. I heard Mrs. Wilmont start playing "BEAUTIFUL DREAMER."

Liz, Max, and Johnny rushed over to help me lie down and stick my head out of the hole in the front orange crate.

"That Mutt and Jeff out there killed any chance for me to win the Super Treat Basket," Max said.

"Hey, you handled them great!" I exclaimed.

"I'm dead in the water, too," Johnny groaned.

"Dave, what about the pie?" Liz asked.

"I'll think of something," I promised. *"That is one pie that is not going to go to waste!"*

"I hope you win," Johnny said, helping to push my two FAKE feet out through the holes in the bottom crate. I checked the skateboards beneath me and pulled my real legs up against my chest so the top of the crate could close.

"Are you okay, pal?" Johnny asked.

"Yes," I said.

"Good luck," Liz said.

"Double good luck," Max added.

The only member of the Wacky Facts Lunch Bunch not there with me was Jennifer. I saw her in a corner warming up her dance with Pecky Barnes.

Nat Bronski screeched, "Dave, Mrs. Wilmont wants you out there NOW!"

"Stand clear!" I yelled, setting the saw on top of the crates so it looked really shiny and scary against the purple shower curtain.

I stuck out my hands and pushed myself along the floor out onto the stage. I know I looked like a turtle on its back, but I wanted that as part of the shock effect. The entire audience gawked as I turned my head and spoke into the mike on the floor.

"FOLKS, YOU ARE ABOUT TO WITNESS AN ACT OF MAGIC NEVER ATTEMPTED BEFORE IN THE HISTORY OF THE WORLD! IN FRONT OF YOUR VERY EYES, I WILL NOW PROCEED TO SAW MYSELF IN HALF!"

Mrs. Wilmont kept playing "BEAUTIFUL DREAMER" as I reached up and took the saw. I started sawing at the spot where I had attached the two crates. Of course, my real body was safe in the front box with my knees bent up to my shoulders.

I dragged the sawing out for two minutes like I was really sawing one long coffin in half.

"NOW, LADIES AND GENTLEMEN," I said into the mike, "PLEASE DO NOT MAKE A SOUND, OR SOMETHING HORRIBLE MIGHT HAPPEN!"

I set the saw safely to one side, put my hands on the floor, and shoved with all my might. Both crates went rolling on the skateboards. The problem was, I

had pushed too hard. The crate with me in it went rolling straight toward the feet of Dolly the Witch. The other crate rolled six feet and fell over. One of my fake feet fell out!

"Hey, you want another leg?" Herb shouted. "I got a top-of-the-line one for you!"

Mrs. Wilmont, the whole class, and I shrieked as Herb reached down and took off his left leg. He waved it in the air and started hopping around on the stage.

"Well, what have we here?" the Wicked Witch of the West cackled as she reached down. She found the lid of the crate and lifted it up.

The audience roared when it got a load of me doubled over like an anchovy.

I felt my face flush red-hot.

I stood up and was thankful that Herb was hopping around waving his leg. It gave me a chance to clear my orange crates. I was really freaked out of my mind by the time I set the microphone back up.

"We're next!" Wendy Potts yelled at me from behind the screen.

"I know it!" I called back.

"NOW, FOLKS, FOR YOUR ENTERTAINMENT PLEASURE, THE ONE AND ONLY DOO WAH GIRLS!"

Wendy Potts and the rest of the Stuck-ups scooted on stage. Mrs. Wilmont played the piano as they sang:

We're in love with Bobby,
Doo wah, doo wah,
Bobby thrills us so,
Doo wah, doo wah . . .

I was so whacked out I barely made it back behind the screen. I almost sat on the hatbox by mistake as I sank to the floor.

"It wasn't so bad," Liz said, sitting next to me. "It was funny."

"Yes," Max agreed, getting down on one knee.

"I think a lot of people really enjoyed it," Johnny said. "They really enjoyed Herb hopping around on one leg."

I did not even want to speak. It felt good having my pals around me. The only thing more I could have asked for was Jennifer's coming over so the WFLB could all suffer together.

"At least the DOO WAH number is long," I said. "I really need the time to rest."

"I know what you mean," Liz said.

"There is that CLICKING again," Max said.

"It is SO annoying," Liz groaned. "I can't tell you how much I was distracted when I was singing. My only memory of singing 'MEMORIES' is CLICKING!"

"What is Isabel doing out there?" Johnny said. The CLICKING got louder and faster.

We all stood up and peeked out from behind the screen, because the CLICKING began to sound like a machine gun. Isabel Zaks was on her feet, tap-dancing toward the DOO WAH GIRLS.

"Pick up the beat!" Isabel called out to Mrs. Wilmont.

Before anyone knew what was happening, Isabel was standing in front of Wendy Potts and the Stuck-ups, tap-dancing up a storm. As the audience began to clap, Isabel started to do twirls. Then kicks! Her taps were so loud the DOO WAH GIRLS were going off pitch.

Suddenly, Estelle was on her feet, heading for the stage. She began to stomp in her cowgirl boots, and her frills bounced. I noticed Mrs. Wilmont's mouth drop open when Estelle burst into song. In her booming voice she joined right in singing, "WE'RE IN LOVE WITH BOBBY, DOO WAH, DOO WAH . . ."

Helen, the lady with the bleached blond hair, stood up next and called to the audience, "Come on, everybody, sing!"

As practically everyone in the audience started singing "DOO WAH, DOO WAH," Herb, Sol, and Manny got up and made a line behind the Stuck-ups as if they were backup singers.

"Yoo-hoo, Mrs. Wilmont," Helen called out. "Do you know the song **'A GOOD MAN IS HARD TO FIND'**?"

"NO!" Mrs. Wilmont yelled back in a voice that was not at all polite.

"That's okay," Helen shouted, charging to the piano. "I *DO*!"

Helen practically pushed Mrs. Wilmont off the bench and began pounding the piano with a really jazzy beat. Mrs. Wilmont stood up, her face red as a tomato. She looked really bewildered. Finally, she turned and signaled to all the kids back behind the screen. The Social Committee was singing and dancing up a storm in front of their pals.

"I do not want those show-stealing show-offs to get away with this," Mrs. Wilmont said slowly, deliberately. "If they wanted to do their own show, that's one thing. But they invited our class. That's another."

"What can we do?" Liz asked.

Mrs. Wilmont had to shout over the racket. "We can all stick together and we can take back the stage!"

Supernerd Tommy Russo said, *"You said it was fine to stand out from a crowd. They are standing out."*

"WHEN THE CROWD IS SHOOTING AT YOU, YOU DO SOMETHING—OR IN OTHER WORDS, OUR SHOW MUST GO ON!" Mrs. Wilmont said loud and clear.

"Let's get them, Mrs. Wilmont!" I yelped.

"You lead the charge, Dave," Mrs. Wilmont ordered. *"I want all of our kids to have their chance to perform. I do not give a hoot about that front row of show biz* **HAMS! Oh, my goodness—I can't believe I just said that about kind senior citizens!"**

NINE

Splaaaaaaaaaaat!

I ran back onstage.

Mrs. Wilmont headed for the piano. I fought my way past the fleeing Stuck-ups and the dancing, singing Social Committee.

Estelle clutched the microphone. She was still singing "DOO WAH, DOO WAH," but to Helen's "A GOOD MAN IS HARD TO FIND."

"Excuse me," I said as I took the mike right out of her hands.

"Hey, we're in the middle of a great song!" Estelle boomed.

"So were we," I said to her, and then I yelled into the mike, "AND NOW, LADIES AND GENTLEMEN, THE FIFTH GRADE IS PROUD TO PRESENT ONE OF ITS FINEST ACTS!" I didn't even know which one it should be.

Mrs. Wilmont reached the piano bench.

"Pardon me," she told Helen as she slid back onto the bench, forcing her off the keyboard.

"YOU'RE ALL GOING TO LOVE THIS NEXT PERFORMANCE!" Mrs. Wilmont announced as her hands started playing loud chords.

"IT IS GOING TO BE GREAT!" I blasted into the mike.

The Social Committee looked curious.

"SIT DOWN, EVERYONE! SIT DOWN!" *I* was giving the orders now.

The Committee stopped dancing and singing and finally sat down in their chairs. I looked to Mrs. Wilmont to see if she had a clue as to what act we should put on next. She looked back at me and shrugged her shoulders just as I heard Pecky's grating voice shoot out from behind the screen.

"It *is* my turn to M.C., you know, Dave."

I ignored her.

"AND SO, LADIES AND GENTLEMEN, HERE IS THE NEXT ACT . . ." I thought fast. We still had the Jocks who RAP, and the Zombies, and John Quinn was set to play the violin.

The Bride of Frankenstein headed out on the stage right for me.

"Give me that mike," Pecky demanded.

"OUR NEXT ACT IS THE KANGAROO HIP HOP!" I yelled into the mike.

"It is *not*!" Pecky screeched. She was so furious

even the cinder block of red hair on top of her head shook.

"IT GIVES ME GREAT PLEASURE TO INTRO-DUCE REBECCA BARNES AND JENNIFER LO-PEZ!" I announced.

Jennifer came out onto the stage and stood next to Pecky. In their red, white, and blue costumes they looked like a couple of American flags.

"We are not going to do THE KANGAROO HIP HOP now!" Pecky yelled, grabbing my arm and squeezing it hard. "We are saving it to close the show!"

I looked at Jennifer. She looked at me.

"Please do it now. We need it," I asked.

"All right, Dave," Jennifer said.

"It's not all right!" Pecky screamed.

"MAESTRO, PLEASE," I called to Mrs. Wilmont. She started playing THE KANGAROO HIP HOP music.

Jennifer began dancing and singing. Pecky had no choice but to join in. **"DO THE KANGAROO! DO THE KANGAROO! LISTEN AND I'LL SHOW YOU HOW TO DO THE KANGAROO! FIRST YOU ROCK IT TO THE LEFT, THEN YOU ROLL IT TO THE RIGHT . . . !"**

I cleared out of the way as Pecky and Jennifer started HIP HOPPING. Maybe the Jocks would have been better next. I figured I had probably made a mistake. I looked at the front row. The entire Social Committee was riveted on THE KANGA-ROO HIP HOP, and the rest of the audience looked like they were enjoying it, too. The first row started to sway a bit. Isabel began her CLICKING again. I could not believe we had actually managed to take back the show.

"THEN YOU HIP HOP! HIP HOP! WITH ALL YOUR MIGHT!"

Sol, Murray, and Herb were the first ones to start clapping along with the song. Naturally, Isabel started to tap-dance. Helen and Estelle joined in the singing. The whole audience started having a really great time. The only one with a sour puss was Pecky.

Suddenly, I realized what would be even more fun. I ran out and got in front of Pecky so now there were three of us HIP HOPPING.

"What are you doing?" Pecky sneered.

"We should let everybody join in like that Conga line you told me about," I said.

Pecky growled now. "This dance is just Jennifer and me. We're going to win the Super Treat Basket! We're going to have our picture in the newspaper!"

"ONE, TWO, THREE—KICK!" I called into the mike. It felt like it fit in perfectly with the HIP HOP-PING!

"Stop it!" Pecky yelled, trying to stay as the loco-motive in a train of two.

I kept jumping in front of her so I was at the head of the line.

"COME ON, EVERYBODY!" I shouted into the mike. "DO THE KANGAROO!"

It took exactly one second before Isabel tap-danced her way right behind Jennifer and held on to her hips. Murray, Sol, Helen, Estelle, and Herb lined up.

"Stop them!" Pecky ordered me.

"Why?"

"This is Jennifer's and my act!"

"Not anymore," I said. I kept reaching behind me, trying to make Pecky put her hands on my hips.

I turned to look at her face. "I hate you!" Pecky gritted her teeth as she HOPPED. She was really trembling. Maybe I had gone too far.

But at least twenty other senior citizens came up from the audience and joined in. The chant became **"HIP HOP, ONE, TWO, THREE—KICK! HIP HOP . . . !"**

I suppose what really pushed Pecky over the edge was when Herb with the beer belly and fake leg came to center stage. He pulled his T-shirt up to show he had painted a big face on his huge belly. He joined the piano music and started whistling THE KANGAROO **HIP** HOP and moving his belly so it looked like it was really his belly button that was whistling.

Pecky had had it. She rushed off the stage and ran behind the screen. Jennifer put her arms on my waist, and we just kept THE KANGAROO line going. I was having so much fun I did not notice Pecky heading back onstage. By the time I saw her she was running at me at full speed with the pie in her left hand.

"I will fix you, Dave Martin!" Pecky screamed and really got my attention, so that as she threw the pie right at me, I ducked.

The pie smacked the side of my head, but most of it bounced SPLAT into Jennifer's face!

The audience roared with laughter.

Jennifer stopped dancing.

"I'm so sorry," Pecky called to Jennifer.

Jennifer lifted her hands to her face. It took her a long time for her to find her eyes. When she brought her hands down, they were filled with huge clumps of whipped cream.

"Oh, Jennifer"—the Bride of Frankenstein suddenly started laughing—"you look like a melting snowman!"

A growl came out from the lump of cream that was Jennifer's head. Pecky must have heard the growl, too, because she started to back off, but not before Jennifer thrust the giant clumps of white stuff at Pecky.

I grabbed some of the cream off my head and threw it at Pecky, too, but Pecky ducked, and it hit

Murray. Murray howled with laughter as he grabbed a handful of cream from the floor and threw it at Isabel. It was like an atomic reaction. Before anyone knew what was going on, the Social Committee was throwing whipped cream at each other. Everyone howled with laughter, and Mrs. Wilmont kept playing THE KANGAROO HIP HOP with a weird expression on her face.

I poked Jennifer in the ribs and said, "We're a hit!"

"This turned into what you wanted," Jennifer agreed, "a LAUGH RIOT!"

Punch Line!

By the time the **KANGAROO HIP HOP** was over and all the whipped cream was cleaned up, everyone in the audience was exhausted. Even the Social Committee behaved themselves for the rest of the talent show. The Jocks' rap went great. Richard Wood did such a great job leading the Zombies in their poetry recital that they actually seemed alive. The girl Jocks' precision basketball dribbling routine to "STARS AND STRIPES FOREVER" was really stirring. Even the nerds did okay with their LYING GAME. The surprise hit of the show was John Quinn playing the violin. The senior citizens were quiet and really applauded for him.

    "WELL, LADIES AND GENTLEMEN," Mrs.

Wilmont announced at the end, **"THAT'S OUR SHOW!"**

The whole class came out onstage, and the audience gave us a big round of applause as they stood up. It made all of us feel really great—except the Bride of Frankenstein, of course.

"And let's hear it for Mrs. Wilmont!" I shouted.

"Yea!" Johnny led the cheers.

Everybody applauded Mrs. Wilmont like crazy. Her face turned really rosy as we all ran off the stage and surrounded her.

"Who wins the Super Treat Basket and gets their picture in the paper?" Pecky asked flat out.

"That's not what is important." Mrs. Wilmont lowered her voice so only the class could hear. "What I hope we have all learned today is that individually we all have talent—but together we're even stronger!"

"Dave ruined my act," Pecky wailed.

"Hey, it was my act, too, you know," Jennifer reminded her. "And he did not ruin it—he improved it!"

Mrs. Wilmont put her arm on my shoulder. "What Dave did was stop us from being creamed," she said. "He and Jennifer and Max—all of you, including Becky—showed us you have what it takes to make it in life. You were able to think on your feet! That is what survival on this planet is really all about! It doesn't matter who wins any prize. You've all won! Congratulations to all of you!"

Isabel Zaks stood up and CLICKED her way to the microphone. I should have known something unexpected was going to happen when I didn't see any of the Social Committee comparing notes or voting on the acts. How were they going to pick the winner?

"Mrs. Wilmont—and most worthy performers," Isabel said to us. **"As you may have noticed, most of us on the Social Committee have had professional experience in show business. At a special meeting yesterday, we unanimously decided that we would not be able to pick a single winner of today's talent show . . ."**

"What is she talking about?" Liz whispered.

"I don't know," I said.

"Did she say they weren't going to give out any prize?" Max asked.

Isabel pointed to Dolly the Witch standing at the back of the room. "What I am trying to say is . . . THIS!"

Dolly pulled open a sliding partition. There stood Sol, Murray, Estelle, Herb, and Helen. They pushed forward a cart heaped high with a humongous pile of Treat Baskets.

"Look at all the baskets!" Liz cried out.

"What's going on?" Wendy Potts asked.

Isabel laughed. "The Social Committee decided you would all be winners for coming to perform for us today. Each of you has won a Super Treat Basket."

The class gasped.

Isabel led us all to the cart. As the Social Committee handed us each a basket, a photographer started flashing with his camera. Isabel Zaks had arranged this publicity, and we were all going to have our picture in the newspaper! Each basket had homemade fudge and cookies and hand-dipped chocolates and a whole coupon book of movie passes. Even Mrs. Wilmont got one.

"This must have really cut into their Social Security checks," I said to Liz.

"THANK YOU!" Mrs. Wilmont called out to everyone.

"THANK YOU!" the class sang out.

Estelle sat down at the piano. She started playing "ROCK AROUND THE CLOCK" for us to march out to. All the senior citizens reached out to shake our hands.

"Good-bye, Herb!"

"Good-bye, Sol and Murray!"

"Good-bye, Estelle and Isabel and Helen and Dolly."

As we carried our Super Treat Baskets out past our new old friends, the newspaper photographer took more parting shots of us. I thought of how glad

I was all of the members of the WFLB were together again.

"We're friends until death do us part!" I whispered to my pals.

"Right on!" they cheered. **"Right on!"**

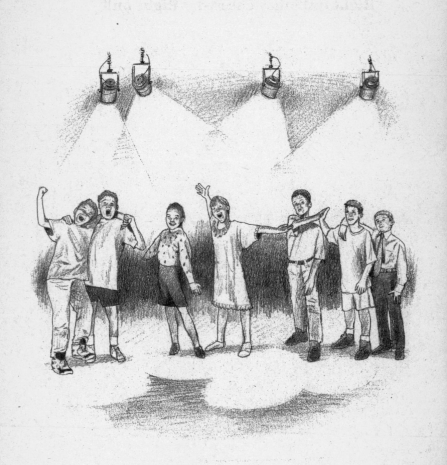

The Wacky Facts Lunch Bunch wants YOU to
GROSS US OUT!!

We know that when you're in the school cafeteria you are *re-pulsive, disgusting,* and *utterly slimy.*

WHY??

Because of the cafeteria food!!

Now is your chance to send us your grossest lunch experience. We've already heard the one about your egg salad sandwich getting smashed into your chocolate cake and how you were so hungry you ate it anyway!!!

And the chocolate-covered ants that tasted so good!

YOU CAN TOP THAT.

Write down your grossest gross-out experience and send it with your name and address to:

GROSS-OUT LUNCH CONTEST
Bantam Doubleday Dell BFYR
1540 Broadway
New York, NY   10036

Gross us out and win some FREE books!

OFFICIAL CONTEST RULES

1. NO PURCHASE NECESSARY TO ENTER OR RECEIVE THE PRIZE. To enter the Gross-Out Lunch Contest, write your name and address on a piece of paper and attach a true, humorous story of 100 words or less. Mail your entry to: GROSS-OUT LUNCH CONTEST,

Bantam Doubleday Dell BFYR, 1540 Broadway, New York, NY 10036. Limit two entries per person. All entries must be received by April 1, 1994, to be considered eligible. Illegible entries will not be accepted. We are not responsible for late, lost, or misdirected entries, and all entries become the property of BDD and will not be returned.

PHOTOCOPIES OR MECHANICALLY REPRODUCED ENTRIES ARE NOT ACCEPTABLE.

2. All entries meeting the above-mentioned criteria will be read and considered by a panel of judges, and the best entry (based on its editorial merits) will be selected as the winner. Winner will be selected on or about June 1, 1994. Decision of the judges will be final and binding. Winner will be notified by mail and will be required to execute an affidavit of eligibility and release that must be signed by winner and winner's parent or legal guardian and returned within 14 days of notification. In the event of noncompliance with this time period, an alternate winner will be chosen.

3. ONE PRIZE as follows: One or more boxes of books published by Bantam Doubleday Dell Books for Young Readers. Approximate value of the prize: $100.00. No prize substitution or transfer allowed.

4. This contest is open only to the residents of the U.S. and Canada, excluding the province of Quebec, who are between the ages of 6 and 15 at the time of entry. Employees of Bantam Doubleday Dell Publishing Group, Inc. and its affiliates and subsidiaries and their immediate family members are not eligible. Void where prohibited or restricted by law. Taxes, if any, are the sole responsibility of the winner.

5. Entering the contest constitutes permission for use of the winner's name, photo, or likeness, and biographical data for publicity and promotional purposes on behalf of BDD, with no additional compensation.

6. For the name of the winner, available after June 31, 1994, send a stamped, self-addressed envelope, entirely separate from your entry, to Bantam Doubleday Dell BFYR, 1540 Broadway, New York, NY 10036.

Attack of the Killer Fishsticks
Team up with Action Dave and the Wacky Facts Lunch Bunch for their first mind-boggling adventure!

My name is Dave Martin and I'm president of the WACKY FACTS LUNCH BUNCH. My three best friends and I formed our club on the first day of school. Just like in most schools, the kids split up into different groups in the lunchroom. Liz, Johnny, Jennifer, and I don't fit into the Stuck-ups, the Brains, the Supernerds, the Zombies, or the Jocks. And we certainly weren't going to sit with the Nasty Blobs. The Nasty Blobs is our code name for Nat Bronski and Rado Clapp—the two most rotten, creepy, mean goons in our fifth grade class. They may be only two kids, but they are bonkers enough for a whole nuthouse.

Fright Party
It's almost Halloween and the Wacky Facts Lunch Bunch are planning the spookiest party ever . . . and you're invited!

"Well," Jennifer replied, "I went to a party once and here's what they did. Before the party they put grapes in a pan and covered them with slimy egg whites, so that when we touched them in a dark room they felt just like *eyeballs.*"

Liz scrunched up her face.

"My mother makes homemade noodles. When they're raw, I tease my brothers because the noodles are so slippery. I could put them in a bowl and we could say they were *vampire brains,*" Johnny suggested.

"Great," I said.

"Great?" Liz yelled in disbelief. "It's disgusting."

"That's the point," Johnny said, smiling.

Fifth Grade Safari

Join the Wacky Facts Lunch Bunch as they head out on a wild and freaky fifth grade safari!

It was the first time any of us in the WACKY FACTS LUNCH BUNCH had been to the zoo since it had been restructured and made into a whole fantastic habitat.

"There aren't any more cages!" Jennifer said. "I'm glad about that. I used to think it was mean to put animals in prison."

"Me too," Max said. "Now they have moats and log fences and vines."

Everything's so natural," I agreed. "It's like we're on safari in a real jungle!"

"The monkeys really look happy!" Johnny said, making goofy faces and grunting sounds at them.

"They think you're bonkers," Jennifer moaned, turning the camcorder on a couple of baboons who swung from branches and screeched.

"They're so cute," Liz said.

"They're gross," a voice suddenly growled. It was Nat. The Nasty Blobs had followed us. They always try to stick their noses into anything we do.

"All monkeys do is pick nits off each other," Nat babbled on.

"They do not," Liz defended them. "What do you know anyway?"

"They *love* nits," Rado squeaked.

We all turned to take a closer look at the monkeys. A lot of them *were* picking things off one another's heads.

"Monkeys just *groom* each other," I explained. "I read that in a *National Geographic* magazine."

"Yeah, Dave, I figured you'd know all about nits. Isn't that monkey on the left your cousin?" Nat howled.

"Buzz off," I told him.